W9-DDM-056

AUG 2005

NORMAN BRIDWELL
Clifford's
HALLOWEEN

Story and pictures by Norman Bridwell

SCHOLASTIC INC.
New York

NORTHPORT PUBLIC LIBRARY
NORTHPORT. NEW YORK

To the real Emily Elizabeth's real friends:
Alison and Andrew
Melissa
Carolyn
Christian
Kate
and Mrs. Gallagher

No part of this publication may be reproduced in whole or in part, or stored in a retrieval system,
or transmitted in any form, or by any means, electronic, mechanical, photocopying, recording, or
otherwise, without written permission of the publisher. For information regarding permission, write to
Scholastic Inc., 555 Broadway, New York, NY 10012.

ISBN 0-590-96337-6

Copyright © 1986, 1966 by Norman Bridwell.
All rights reserved. Published by Scholastic Inc.
CLIFFORD and CLIFFORD THE BIG RED DOG are registered trademarks of Norman Bridwell.

12 11 10 9 8 7 6 5 4 3 2   9   6 7 8 9/9 0 1/0
Printed in the U.S.A.   24

I'm Emily Elizabeth.
Today is a holiday! It's my favorite day of the year.

This is my dog, Clifford.
Today is his favorite day, too.

With a big red dog like Clifford, every day is fun. But holidays are the most fun of all.

At Christmas, Clifford makes a very good Santa.
He already has a red coat.

And on New Year's Eve, we stay up until midnight
so Clifford can blow his New Year's horn —

Happy New Year.

On Valentine's day —

— Clifford is my favorite valentine.

And you should see Clifford on Easter.
He makes a wonderful Easter bunny.

On April Fool's Day,
Clifford never plays tricks on anyone . . .

and no one plays tricks on Clifford.

On Thanksgiving, Clifford gets a great big turkey.

But today is the best holiday of all —

HALLOWEEN!

Last year we had a big Halloween party.
I dressed as a pirate, but I didn't know
how to dress Clifford.

Daddy thought Clifford would make a good devil.

I wanted him
to be a clown . . .

or maybe a witch.

But Clifford wanted to be —

a ghost.

When the children came to the party, nobody could guess who the big ghost really was.

We had fun.
We bobbed for apples.

Clifford wanted to play, too.

We played another game with apples.

Clifford won that game.

Then Mommy told us a ghost story.
But we weren't afraid . . . .

We had the biggest ghost on our street
taking care of us.

After the party, Clifford and I
went trick-or-treating.

We didn't have much luck.
But we didn't mind.

It was time to go to bed anyhow.
Halloween was over.

And now Halloween has come again.
I am not going to be a pirate this year.
I am going to be a fairy princess.

But what should Clifford be?

An Indian?

A knight?

What do you suggest?